The
Who Wa
GW00726887

The Boy Who Wanted a Dog

Enid Blyton

Pictures by Gareth Floyd

The publishers would like to thank Beachie Bagenal, Julia Cook, Hannah Cook, and Molly and her puppies for their enthusiasm and participation in the photographic shoot for this cover.

The Boy Who Wanted a Dog was first published by
Lutterworth Press in 1963
First Published by Bloomsbury Publishing Plc in 1997
38 Soho Square, London W1V 5DF

Enid Blyton™

A CIP catalogue record of this book is available from the British Library

ISBN 0 7475 3213 3

Printed in Great Britain by Clays Ltd, St Ives plc

10 9 8 7 6 5 4 3 2 1

Cover design by Mandy Sherliker

CONTENTS

CHAPTER 1
When Granny Came to Tea

'Hello, Granny!' said Donald, rushing in from afternoon school. 'I hope you've come to tea!'

'Yes, I have!' said Granny. 'And I've come to ask you a question, too. It's your birthday soon – what would you like me to give you?'

'He really doesn't deserve a birthday present,' said his father, looking up from his paper. 'His weekly reports from school haven't been good.'

'Well, Dad – I'm not brainy like you,' said Donald, going red. 'I do try. I really do. But arithmetic beats me, I just *can't* do it. And I just hate trying to write essays and things – I can't seem to think of a thing to say!'

'You *can* work if you want to,' said his mother, beginning to pour out the tea. 'Look what your master said about your nature work – "Best work in the whole form. Knows more about birds and animals than anyone." Well, why can't you do well at writing and arithmetic!'

'They're not as interesting as nature,' said Donald. 'Now, when we have lessons about dogs and horses and squirrels and birds, I don't miss a word! And I write jolly good essays about *them*!'

'Did you get good marks today?' asked his father.

Donald shook his head, and his father frowned. 'I suppose you sat dreaming as usual!' he said.

'Well – geography was so dull this morning that I somehow couldn't keep my mind on it,' said Donald. 'It was all about things called peninsulas and isthmuses.'

'And what *were* you keeping your mind on – if it happened to be working?' asked his father.

'Well – I was thinking about a horse I saw when I was going to school this morning,' said Donald, honestly.

'But why think of a *horse* in your geography lesson?' said his mother.

'Well, Mother – it was a nice old horse, and doing its best to pull a heavy cart,' said Donald. 'And I couldn't help noticing that it had a dreadful sore place on its side, that was being rubbed by the harness. And oh, Mother, instead of being sorry for the horse, the man was hitting it!'

'And so you thought of the horse all through your geography lesson?' said Granny, gently.

'Well, I couldn't help it,' said Donald. 'I kept wondering if the man would put something on the sore place, when he got the horse home. I kept thinking what *I* would do if it were my horse. Granny, people who keep animals should be kind to them, and notice when they are ill or hurt, shouldn't they?'

'Of course they should,' said Granny. 'Well, don't worry about the horse any more. I'm sure the man has tended it by now. Let's talk of something happier. What would you like for your birthday?'

'Oh Granny – there's something I want more than anything else in the world!' said Donald, his eyes shining.

'Well, if it's not *too* expensive and is possible to get, you shall have it!' said Granny. 'What is it?'

'A puppy!' said Donald, in an excited voice. 'A puppy of my very own! I can make him a kennel myself. I'm good with my hands, you know!'

'*No*, Donald!' said his mother, at once. 'I will *not* have a dirty little puppy messing about the house, chewing the mats to pieces, rushing about tripping everyone up, and . . .'

'He wouldn't! He wouldn't!' said Donald. 'I'd train him well. He'd walk at my heels. He could sleep in my bedroom on a rug. He could . . .'

'Sleep in your room! Certainly not!' said his mother quite shocked. 'No, Granny – *not* a puppy, please. Donald's bad enough already, the things he brings home – caterpillars, a hedgehog – ugh, the prickly thing – a stray cat that smelt dreadful and stole the fish out of the larder – and . . .'

'Oh Mother – I wouldn't bring *any*thing into the house if only you'd let me have a puppy!' said Donald. 'It's the thing I want most in the world. A puppy of my very own! Granny, please, please give me one.'

'NO,' said his father. 'You don't *deserve* a puppy while your school work is so bad. Sorry, Granny. You'll have to give him something else.'

Granny looked sad. 'Well, Donald – I'll give you some books about animals,' she said. 'Perhaps your father will let you have a puppy when you get a fine school report.'

'I never will,' said poor Donald. 'I'm not nearly as clever as the other boys, except with my hands. I'm making you a little foot-stool, Granny, for *your* birthday. I'm carving a pattern all round it – and the woodwork master said that even *he* couldn't have done it better. I'm good with my hands.'

'You've something else that is good too,' said Granny. 'You've a good heart, Donald, and a kind one. Well, if you mayn't have a puppy for your birthday, you must come with me to the bookshop and choose some really lovely books. Would you like one about dogs – and another about horses, or cats?'

'Yes. I'd like those very much,' said Donald. 'But oh – how I'd *love* a puppy.'

'Let's change the subject,' said his father. 'What about tea? I see Mother has made some of her chocolate cakes for you, Granny. Donald, forget this puppy business, please, and take a chair to the table for Granny.'

So there they all are, sitting at the tea-table,

eating jam sandwiches, chocolate buns and biscuits. Donald isn't talking very much. He is thinking hard – 'dreaming', as his teacher would say.

'Where would I keep the puppy if I had one?' he thinks. 'Let me see – I could make a dear little kennel, and put it in my own bit of garden. How pleased the puppy would be to see me each morning. What should I call him – Buster? Scamper? Wags? Barker? No – he mustn't bark, Mother would be cross. I'll teach him to . . .'

'Look! Donald's dreaming again!' said his mother. 'Wake up, Donald! Pass Granny the buns! I wonder what you're dreaming about *now*!'

Granny knew! She smiled at him across the table. Dear Donald! *Why* couldn't she give him the puppy that he so much wanted?

CHAPTER 2

All Because of a Kitten

Two days later Donald had quite an adventure! It was all because of a kitten. He was walking home from school, swinging his satchel, and saying 'Hello' to all the dogs he met, when he suddenly saw a kitten run out of a front gate. It was a very small one, quite black, fluffy and round-eyed.

'I'll have to take that kitten back into its house, or it will be run over!' thought Donald, and began to run. But someone else had seen it too – the dog across the road. Ha – a kitten to chase! What fun!

And across the road sped the dog, barking. The kitten was terrified, and tried to run up a nearby tree – but it wasn't in time to escape the dog, who stood with his forepaws on the trunk of the tree, snapping at the kitten's tail and barking.

'Stop it! Get down!' shouted Donald, racing up. 'Leave the kitten alone!'

The dog raced off. Donald looked at the terrified kitten, clinging to the tree-trunk. Was it hurt?

He picked it gently off the tree and looked at it. 'You poor little thing – the dog has bitten your tail – it's bleeding. Whatever can I do? I'll just take you into the house nearby and see if you belong there.'

But no – the woman there shook her head. 'It's not *our* kitten. I don't know who it belongs to. It's been around for some time, and nobody really wants it. That's why it's so thin, poor mite.'

'What a shame!' said Donald, stroking the frightened little thing. It cuddled closer to him, digging its tiny claws into his coat, holding on tightly. It gave a very small mew.

'Well – I'd better take it home,' thought Donald. 'I can't possibly leave it in the street. That dog would kill it if he caught it! But whatever will Mother say? She doesn't like cats.'

He tucked it gently under his coat and walked home, thinking hard. What about that old tumble-down shed at the bottom of the garden? He could put a box there with an old piece of cloth in it for the kitten – and somehow he could manage to make the door shut so that it would be safe.

'You see, your tail is badly bitten,' he said to the kitten, whose head was now peeping out of his coat. 'You can't go running about with such a hurt tail. I'll have to get some ointment and a bandage.'

Donald thought he had better not take the kitten into the house. There might be a fuss. So he took the little thing straight to the old shed at the bottom of the garden. He saw an old sack there and put it into a box. Then he put the kitten there, and stroked it, talking in the special voice he kept for animals – low and kind and comforting. The kitten gave a little purr.

'Ah – so you can purr, you poor little thing! I shouldn't have thought there was a purr left in you, after your fright this morning!' said Donald. 'Now I'm going to find some ointment and a bandage – and some milk perhaps!'

He shut the shed door carefully, and put a big stone across the place where there was a hole at the bottom. Then he went down to the house. 'Is that you, Donald?' called his mother. 'Dinner will be ready in ten minutes.'

Ten minutes! Good! There would be time to find what he wanted and go quickly back to the shed. He ran into the kitchen, which was empty – his mother was upstairs. Quickly he went to the cupboard where medicines and ointments were kept, and took out a small pot and a piece of lint.

Then he took an old saucer, went to the larder, and poured some milk into it. He tiptoed out of the kitchen door into the garden, thankful that no one had seen him.

Up to the old shed he went. The kitten was lying peacefully in the box, licking her bitten tail.

'I wouldn't use your rough little tongue on that sore place,' said Donald. 'Let me put some ointment on it. It will feel better then. Perhaps it's a good thing, really, you've licked it – it's your way of washing the hurt place clean, I suppose. Now, keep still – I won't hurt you!'

And very gently, he took the kitten on to his knee and stroked it. It began to purr. Donald dipped his finger into the ointment and rubbed it gently over the bitten place. The kitten gave a sudden yowl of pain and almost leapt off his knee!

'Sorry!' said Donald, stroking it. 'Now keep still while I wrap this bit of lint round your tail, and tie it in place.'

The kitten liked Donald's soft, gentle voice. It lay still once more, and let the boy put on the piece of lint – but when he tied it in place, it yowled again, and this time managed to jump right off his knee to the ground!

Donald had put the saucer of milk down on the floor when he had come to the shed, and the kitten suddenly saw it. It ran to it in surprise, and began to lap eagerly, forgetting all about its hurt tail.

The boy was delighted. He had bound up the bitten tail, and had given the kitten milk – the two things he had come to do. He bent down and stroked the soft little head.

'Now you keep quiet here, in your box,' he said. 'I'll come and see you as often as I can.'

He opened the door while the kitten was still lapping its milk, shut it, and went up the garden. He was happy. He liked thinking about the tiny creature down in the shed. It was his now. It was a shame that nobody had wanted it or cared for it. What a pity his mother didn't like cats! If she had loved it, it could have had such a nice home.

'I'll have to find a home for it,' he thought. 'I'll get its tail better first, and then see if I can find someone who would like to have it!'

The kitten drank a little more milk, climbed back into its box, sniffed at the lint round its tail, and went sound asleep. Sleep well, little thing – you are safe for the night!

CHAPTER 3
A Job for Donald

It was not until the next morning that Donald found a chance to slip down to the shed to see the kitten. He took some more milk with him, and a few scraps.

'It will be so hungry!' he thought. 'What a good thing I left it some milk!'

But the milk had hardly been touched, and the kitten was lying very still in its box. It gave a faint mew when Donald bent over it, as if to say, 'Here's that kind boy again!'

'You don't look well, little kitten,' said Donald, surprised. 'What's the matter? You haven't lapped up the milk I left!'

He knew what the matter was when he saw the kitten's tail. It was very swollen, and the tiny creature had torn off the bandage with its teeth! It was in pain, and looked up at the boy as if to say '*Please* help me!'

'Oh dear – something has gone wrong with your poor little tail!' said Donald. 'Perhaps the wound has gone bad, like my finger did when I gashed it on a tin. *Now* what am I to do with you?'

The kitten lay quite still, looking up at Donald. 'I can't take you indoors,' said the boy. 'My mother doesn't like cats. I think I'd better take you to the vet. You needn't be frightened. He's an animal doctor, and he loves little things like you. He'll make your tail better, really he will!'

'Mew-ew!' said the kitten, faintly, glad to see this boy with the kind voice and gentle hands. It cried out when he lifted it up and put it under his coat.

'Did I hurt your poor tail?' said Donald. 'I couldn't help it. If we go quickly I'll have time to take you to the vet's as soon as he's there. It's a good thing it's Saturday, else I would have had to go to school.'

There were already three people in the vet's surgery when Donald arrived – a man with a dog, whose paw was bandaged; a women with a parrot that had a drooping wing; and a small girl with a pet mouse in a box. One by one they were called into the surgery – and at last it was Donald's turn.

The vet was a big man with big hands – hands

that were amazingly gentle and deft. He saw at once that the kitten's tail was in a very bad state.

'It was bitten by a dog,' said Donald. 'I did my best – put ointment on and bound it up.'

'You did well,' said the vet. 'Poor mite! I'm afraid it must lose half its tail. It's been bitten too badly to save. But I don't expect it will worry overmuch at having a short tail!'

'Perhaps the other cats will think it's a Manx cat,' said Donald. 'Manx cats have short tails, haven't they?'

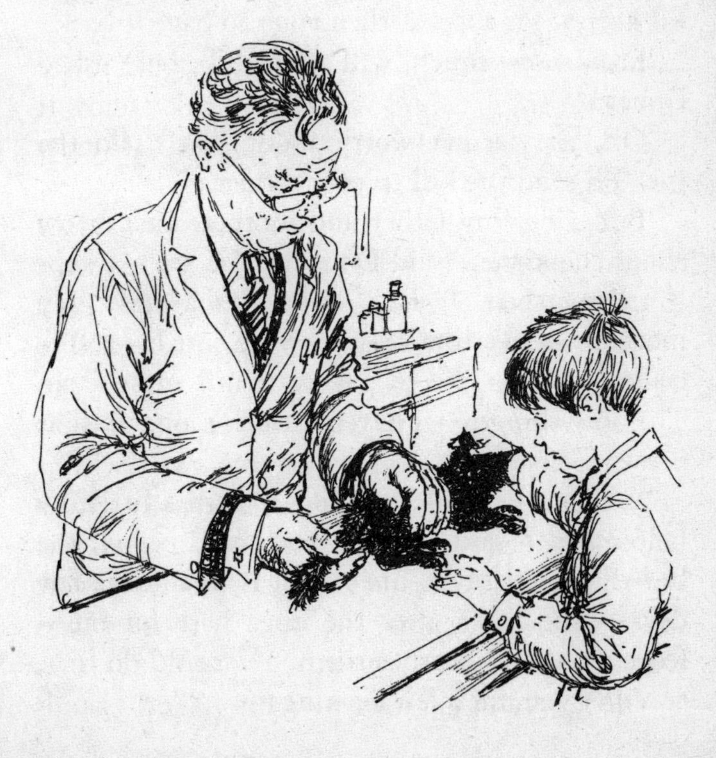

The vet smiled. 'Yes. Now you'll have to leave the kitten with me, and I must deal with its tail. It will be quite all right. It won't be unhappy here.'

Donald liked the vet very much. His big hands held the kitten very gently, and the little thing began to purr.

'Do all animals like you, sir?' he asked.

'Oh yes – animals always know those who are their friends,' he said. 'That kitten knows *you* are its friend. It will let you handle it without fear. I'll keep it for a week, then you can have it back.'

'Er – how much will your bill be?' asked Donald.

'Oh, *you* needn't worry about that!' said the vet. 'I'll send the bill to your father.'

'But, sir – my father and mother don't know about the kitten,' said Donald. 'You see – I kept it in my shed. It isn't mine, it's a stray. My mother doesn't like animals very much – especially cats. I'd like to pay your bill myself, sir. The only thing is – I haven't much money just at present.'

'Well, now, would you like to earn a little, by helping me?' said the vet. 'You could pay off the bill that way! My kennel-maid is away for a few days – she looks after the dogs here for me – feeds them and brushes them. *You* could do that, couldn't you, for a few evenings?'

'Oh YES! Yes, I could,' said Donald, really delighted. 'I'd *love* to. But would you trust me to do the job properly, sir? We've never had a dog at home. But I love dogs, I really do.'

'I'd trust any boy with any animal here, if he handled a kitten as gently as you do,' said the vet. 'It isn't everyone who has the gift of understanding animals, you know. You're lucky!'

'My Granny says that anyone who loves animals understands them,' said Donald.

'She's right,' said the vet. 'Now look – I've more patients waiting for me, as you saw. Leave the kitten in that basket. I'll attend to it as soon as I can. Come back tonight at half-past five, and I'll introduce you to the dogs. Right?'

'Yes, sir,' said Donald, joyfully, and put the kitten gently into the basket on the floor. Then out he went, very happy.

The kitten would be all right now. He could pay the bill by taking the job the vet offered him – and what a job! Seeing to dogs – feeding them – perhaps taking them for walks! But wait a bit – what would his parents say?

He told his father first. 'Daddy, the vet wants a boy to help him a bit while his kennel-maid is away,' said Donald. 'I thought I'd take the job – it's in the evenings – and earn a bit of money. You're always saying that boys are lazy nowadays – not like when you were young, and went out and earned money even while you were at school.'

'Well! I didn't think you had it in you to take a job like that!' said his father. 'I'm pleased. So long as you don't neglect your homework, you can help the vet. Well, well – and I thought you were such a lazy young monkey!'

Donald was delighted. He could hardly wait for the evening to come! Looking after dogs! Would they like him? Would he be able to manage them? Well – he would soon know!

CHAPTER 4

Donald Goes to Work!

Donald could hardly wait for the evening to come. He did his usual Saturday jobs – ran errands for his mother, cleaned his father's bicycle and his own, and weeded a corner of the garden.

Then his mother called him. 'What's this I hear from your father about your working for the vet? You know he's an *animal* doctor? You'll come home all smelly and dirty!'

'I shan't, Mother,' said Donald, in alarm. 'Goodness me, you should see the vet's place – as clean as our own! Anyway, Dad says it will be good for me.'

'Well, if you *do* come home smelling of those animals up at the vet's place, you'll have to give up the job,' said his mother. 'Fancy *wanting* to go and work with animals! I'm surprised at your father letting you!'

Donald kept out of his mother's way all day, really afraid that she would forbid him to go up to the vet's house that evening. He put on his very oldest clothes, and, when at last the clock said a quarter-past-five, off he went at top speed on his bicycle. His first job! And with dogs too! How lucky he was!

He arrived at the vet's, put his bicycle in a shed and went to find the kennels The vet was there, attending to a dog with a crushed paw.

'Ah – you're here already, Donald!' he said. 'Good – you're early, so you can give me a hand with this poor old fellow. He's had such a shock that he's scared stiff. I want to calm him down before I do anything.'

'What happened?' asked Donald, shocked to see the poor, misshapen front paw of the trembling dog.

'It was caught in a door,' said the vet. 'Apparently the wind slammed the door shut, and he couldn't get his paw away in time. He's a nervy dog. Do you think you can hold him still while I examine the paw?'

'I don't know. I'll try,' said Donald. He stroked the dog and spoke to it in his 'special' voice – the one he used for animals. 'Poor old boy – never mind – you'll soon be able to walk on that paw. Poor old boy, then, poor old boy.'

The dog turned to him, pricked its ears, and

listened. Then it licked Donald on the cheek, and gave a little whine of pain.

'Go on talking to him,' said the vet. 'Don't stop. He's listening to you. He won't mind about me if you take his attention.'

So Donald went on talking and stroking, and the dog listened, trying to get as close to the boy as he could. This boy was a comforting boy. This boy had a lovely, clean, boy-smell. He was worth listening to!

The dog gave a little whine now and again as the vet worked on his hurt paw. Soon the vet spoke to him. 'Nearly over now, old dog. I'm putting a plaster on, so don't be afraid. You'll be able to walk all right, your foot will be protected. Nearly over now.'

The dog gave a huge sigh and laid his head on Donald's shoulder. Donald was so happy to feel it there that he could hardly speak to the dog for a moment. He found himself repeating what the vet had said. 'Nearly over now, old dog, nearly over now.'

'Well – that's it,' said the vet, standing up. 'Come on, old dog – to your kennel, now, and a nice long sleep.'

The dog followed him, limping. Donald went too. The dog licked his hand every now and again, as if thanking him. The vet put him into a roomy kennel with straw on the floor, and shut the door. 'Goodnight, old dog!' called Donald, and from the kennel came a short bark – 'Woof-woof!'

'He'll be all right,' said the vet. 'You did well to hold him, youngster – a big dog like that. You have a good voice for animals, too. Now, here are the dogs I want you to brush, and to give fresh water to. Clean up any kennels that need it. You'll find fresh straw yonder if necessary.'

Donald had never had such an interesting

evening in all his life. There were five dogs in the kennels, each in a separate one – and all the dogs were different! He looked at them carefully.

'An alsatian – a labrador – goodness, he's fat – and a corgi with stubby little legs. He looks very intelligent. What's this dog, over in the kennel corner – a little black poodle – what a pet! And this last one – well, goodness knows what it is – a real mixture. A bit of a terrier, a bit of a spaniel, and a bit of something else!'

The dogs barked with joy when the boy came to them. They loved company of any sort and were longing for a walk.

'Three of them are here because their owners are away from home,' said the vet. 'The corgi has a bad ear. The little mongrel ate something he shouldn't and nearly poisoned himself, but he's feeling better now. You won't be scared of going into their kennels, will you? Their bark is worse than their bite!'

'Oh *no*, sir, I'm not scared!' said Donald. 'Shall I take them for a walk when I've finished?'

'Not tonight – we're a bit late,' said the vet. 'I'll take them out myself, last thing. You get on with the brushing.'

He left Donald alone. The boy was too happy for words. He had five dogs to see to – five! And what was more, they all seemed as pleased to see him, as he was to see them!

'Hello, all of you!' he said. 'I'm just going to fetch a can of fresh water for you. Then I'll clean out your kennels, put down fresh straw, and have a word with each of you. Shan't be long.'

And off he went, whistling loudly, to the tap he saw in distance. He filled a large can with water, and went back to the dogs. They were whining and barking now, the bigger ones standing with their paws on the top of their gates.

'I like you all very much,' said Donald, in his 'special' voice. 'I hope you like me too.'

'Woof-woof, WUFF, whine-whine, WOOF-WOOF!' Yes, they certainly liked Donald, no doubt about that. WOOF!

CHAPTER 5

A Wonderful Evening

Donald had a wonderful evening with the five dogs. He went first into the labrador's kennel – it was rather like a small shed with a half-door or gate at the front, to get in by, fastened with a latch on the outer side.

The labrador was a big dog, a lovely golden colour. He stared at Donald in silence as the boy went in. 'Hello!' said Donald. 'How are you? Sorry I don't know your name. I've brought you some fresh water, and I'll sweep out your kennel and give you some fresh straw. Will you like that?'

The labrador lumbered over to the boy and sniffed his legs and hands. Then he wagged his tail slowly. Donald patted him. 'Are you home-sick?' he said. 'Poor old boy! Do you miss your master?'

At the word 'master' the labrador pricked up

his ears and gave a little whine. Donald emptied out the water-bowl, wiped it round with a cloth he had found by the tap, and poured in fresh water. The labrador lapped it eagerly. He didn't like stale water – this was lovely and cold and fresh! He sniffed at Donald again, decided that he liked him, and licked his bare knee.

Donald patted him, delighted. 'Sorry I can't stay long with you,' he said. 'I've the other dogs to see to. But I'll be back to give you a brush-down when I've finished.'

He went to the alsatian's kennel next. This too was a big one, almost a shed. 'Hello!' said Donald. 'My word, you've a big water-bowl – you must be a thirsty dog! Hey, don't drink out of the can, Greedy! That's right – you've plenty in your bowl! I'll come back again soon and brush you.'

The alsatian stopped drinking and went to his gate with Donald, hoping to get out and have a run. 'No, old boy,' said Donald, firmly. 'You'll have to wait for your walk till the vet takes you out tonight. Hey, let me get out of the gate!'

He went to the poodle next, a dear little woolly-coated thing that danced about on tiptoe as soon as the boy came into her kennel. She licked Donald everywhere she could.

'I shall have to bring a towel with me when I come to see *you*,' said Donald. 'You really have a *very* wet tongue. Now – drink your water. I'll be back again in a minute!'

The other two dogs, the corgi and the mongrel, were not feeding very well, especially the corgi, whose ear was hurting him. They wagged their tails and whined when Donald went in to them. The mongrel was very thirsty and drank all his water at once. Donald patted him.

'You're thin,' he said. 'And you look sad. I'll bring your some more water when I come in to clean your kennel.'

The mongrel pressed himself against the boy's legs, grateful for attention and kindness. He whined when Donald went out. That was a nice boy, he thought. He wished he could spend the night with him. He would cuddle up to him and perhaps he would feel better then!

The next thing was to clean out the kennels, and put in fresh straw. Once more the dogs were delighted when Donald appeared, and gave him loud and welcoming barks.

The vet, at work in his surgery, looked out of the window, pleased. The dogs sounded happy. That boy had made friends with them already. Ah, there he was, carrying a bundle of straw!

Donald cleaned out each kennel and put down fresh straw – and the five dogs nuzzled him and whined lovingly while he was in their kennels. He talked to them all the time, and they loved

that. They listened with ears pricked, and gave little wuffs in answer. They gambolled round him, and licked his hand whenever they could. Donald had never felt so happy in all his life.

He had to brush down each dog after he had cleaned the kennels, and this was the nicest job of all. The dogs really loved feeling the firm brushing with the hard-bristled brush. Each dog had his own brush, with his name on it, so to the dogs' delight, Donald suddenly knew their names, and called them by them!

When he had finished his evening's work, he patted each dog and said goodnight. All five dogs stood up with their feet on their gates, watching him go, giving little barks as if to say, 'Come back tomorrow! Do come back!'

'I'll be back!' called Donald, and went up to the surgery to report that he had finished. The vet clapped him on the shoulder and smiled.

'I've never heard the dogs so happy. Well done. Tomorrow is Sunday. Will you be able to come?'

'Oh yes – not in the morning, but I could come in the afternoon and evening, if you've enough jobs for me, sir!' said Donald. 'I'll be glad to earn enough money to pay off the bill for the kitten! Could I see the kitten, sir? Is its tail better?'

'Getting on nicely,' said the vet. 'I've got it in the next room. Come and see it.'

So into the next room they went, and there, in a neat little cage, lying on a warm rug, was the kitten. It mewed with delight when it saw Donald, and stood up, pressing its nose against the cage.

'It only has half a tail now,' said the boy sadly. 'Poor little thing. Is it in pain still?'

'Oh no – hardly at all,' said the vet. 'But I must keep it quiet until the wound has healed.'

'What will happen to it?' asked Donald. 'Nobody will want a kitten with only half a tail, will they? I *wish* my mother would let me keep it.'

'Don't worry about that,' said the vet. 'We'll find a kind home for it. You've done a good evening's work. Come along tomorrow, and you can take the dogs for a walk. I really think I can trust you with the whole lot!'

Donald sped home in delight. As soon as he arrived there, he rushed upstairs, ran a bath for himself, and then put on clean clothes. 'Now Mother won't smell a doggy smell at all!' he thought. 'I just smell of nice clean soap! But oh, *I* think a doggy smell is lovely! I can't wait till tomorrow, I really can't!'

CHAPTER 6

Sunday Afternoon

Donald was very hungry for his supper. He had really worked hard that evening. His mother was surprised to see the amount of bread and butter that he ate with his boiled egg.

'What's made you so hungry?' she asked. 'Oh, of course – you've been helping the vet, haven't you? What did you do?'

'I cleaned out the dog kennels – five of them,' said Donald. 'And I . . .'

'Cleaned out dog kennels! Whatever next?' said his mother, quite horrified.

'Well, I emptied the water-bowls and put in fresh water – and I brushed-down an alsatian called Prince, a labrador, a corgi, a poodle and a mongrel!' said Donald. 'May I have some more bread and butter, please?'

His father began to laugh. 'Boil him another egg, bless him,' he said. 'He's worked harder at the vet's this evening than he ever does at school. It's something to know that he can work well, even if it's just with dogs, and not with books.'

'Well, these dogs are jolly interesting!' said Donald. 'Dad, you should have seen how they all came round me – as if they'd known me for years!'

'That's all very well,' said his mother, 'but I do hope you won't forget your weekend homework in your excitement over these dogs.'

'Gracious! Homework! Oh blow it – I'd forgotten all about it!' said Donald, in dismay. 'It's those awful decimal sums again. I wish I could do sums about *dogs* – I'd soon do those! And I've an essay to write about some island or other – dull as ditch-water. Now, an essay about *dogs* – I could write pages!'

'Just forget about dogs for a bit and finish your supper,' said his mother. 'Then you really must do a little homework.'

'I'm tired now. I'd get all my sums wrong,' said Donald, yawning. 'I'll do it tomorrow morning, before we go to church. I'm going to the vet's again in the afternoon and evening.'

'My word – you *are* keen on your new job!' said his father. 'I'm pleased about that. But I shall stop you going if your school-work suffers, remember.'

Poor Donald! He really was tired that evening

after his work with the dogs. He couldn't do his sums properly. His head nodded forward and he fell asleep. It was a good thing that his parents had gone out! When he awoke it was almost nine o'clock! He hastily put away his undone work and rushed up to bed, afraid that his parents would come in and find his homework still not done.

'I'll have time in the morning!' he thought.

'I'll set my alarm clock and wake early. My mind is nice and clear then!'

So, when his alarm went at seven, he leapt out of bed, and tackled his sums. Yes – they *were* easier to do first thing in the morning. But oh that essay! He'd do that after breakfast. But after breakfast his mother wanted him to do some jobs for her – and then he had to get ready to go to church. That silly essay! What was the sense of writing about something he wasn't at all interested in? If only he could write about those five dogs! Goodness, he would be able to fill pages and pages!

He had told the vet that he would be at the surgery at half-past two. That left him just twenty minutes after midday dinner to do the essay! He took his pen and wrote at top speed, so that his writing was bad and his spelling poor, for he had no time to look up any words in the dictionary.

He looked at the rather smudgy pages when he had finished. His teacher would *not* be pleased. Oh dear – he really hadn't time to do it all over again. Maybe he could wake up early next morning and rewrite it!

Donald changed quickly into his old clothes and rushed out to get his bicycle. Then away he went, pedalling fast, glad that no one had stopped him, and asked him to do a job of some sort!

The boy had a wonderful afternoon. The vet took him into an airy little building where he kept birds that had been hurt, or were ill – and budgerigars that he bred himself for sale. Donald was enchanted with the gay little budgies. The vet let them out of their great cage, and they flew gaily round Donald's head, came to rest on his shoulder or his hand – and one even sat on his ear!

'Oh, how I'd love to breed budgies like these!' he said. 'How I'd like a pair for my own!'

'Good afternoon,' said a voice, suddenly, almost in Donald's ear. 'How are you, how are you, how are you?'

Donald looked round in surprise – and then he laughed. 'Oh – it's that parrot talking!' he said. 'A lovely white parrot! Is he hurt, or something?'

'No. I'm just keeping him for a time because his owner is ill,' said the vet. 'He's a wonderful talker!'

'Shut the door! *Do* shut the door!' said the parrot, and Donald obediently went to the door! The vet laughed.

'Don't shut it! It's just something he knows how to say – one of the scores of things he's always repeating!'

The parrot cleared its throat exactly like Donald's father did. Then it spoke again, in a very cross voice. 'Sit down! Stand up! Go to bed!'

Donald began to laugh – and the parrot laughed too – such a human laugh that the boy was really astonished. Then the vet took him to a shed where he kept any cats that needed his help. The little kitten was there too, curled up asleep, its short tail still bandaged. It looked very happy and contented. There were four big cats there also, one with a bandaged head, one with a leg in plaster.

'All my patients,' said the vet, fondling one of them. 'Cats are more difficult to treat than dogs – not so trusting. Mind that one – she's in pain at the moment, and might scratch you!'

But before the vet had even finished his sentence, Donald was stroking the cat, and talking to it in his 'special' voice. It began to purr loudly, and put down its head for him to scratch its neck.

The vet was amazed. 'Why, that cat will hardly let even *me* touch it!' he said. 'Look, I have to change its bandage now – see if you can hold the cat quiet for me, will you? It fought me like a little fury this morning. Will you risk it? You may be well and truly scratched!'

'I'll risk it,' said Donald, happily. 'I love cats and kittens. Show me what to do, sir – how to hold her. Hark at her purring! *She* won't scratch me!'

Be careful, Donald. Cats are different from dogs. If you go home with your face scratched and torn, you won't be allowed to go and help the vet again. So do be careful.

CHAPTER 7

Donald is Very Busy

'What's the matter with the cat, sir?' asked Donald, as he went on fondling the nervous animal.

'It's hind legs somehow got caught in a trap,' said the vet. 'One has mended well, but the other is badly torn, and won't heal. So I have to paint the leg with some lotion that stings – and this the cat can't bear!'

'How did you manage to hold the cat, and deal with its leg at the same time?' asked Donald, as the cat began to stiffen itself in fright. 'Did the kennel-maid hold it for you when she was here?'

'Oh no – she was frightened of the cat,' said the vet. 'It's half-wild, anyhow – lives in the woods. The keeper brought it to me. It's a lovely cat, really – half Persian. Now – can you hold it. I'll show you how to.'

Gently the vet took the cat and showed the boy how to hold it for him. The cat suddenly spat at him and tried to leap away, her claws out. But the vet's hold was firm and kind.

'I see, sir. I see exactly.' said Donald. 'Poor old puss, then. Don't be scared. We're your friends, you know. Poor old Puss.'

'Go on talking to the cat,' said the vet. 'It's listening to you just like that hurt dog did. You've a wonderful voice for animals. Many children have, if only they knew it – it's a low, kind, soothing voice that goes on and on and animals can't *help* listening. Go on talking to the cat, Donald. It's quieter already.'

The cat struggled a little as Donald held her, talking smoothly and quietly in his 'animal' voice. Soon she lay limp in his hold, and let the vet do what he pleased with her bad leg. She gave a loud yowl once when the lotion suddenly stung, but that was all.

Soon the bandage was on again, and the cat lay quietly in Donald's arms, purring. 'Shall I hold her for a bit, sir?' said the boy. 'She sort of wants comforting, I think.'

The vet looked at the boy holding the wounded cat. 'You know, son, you should be a vet yourself when you grow up!' he said. 'You could do anything with animals! They trust you. How'd you like to be an animal-doctor?'

'I'd like it more than anything in the world!' said Donald. 'I love animals so much – and they love me, sir! They do, really. I've never had a real pet of my own – my parents aren't fond of animals – so I've always had to make do with caterpillars and a hedgehog or two, and once a little wild mouse . . .'

'And I don't suppose you were allowed to bring them into the house, were you?' said the vet. 'Well, some people like animals and everything to do with nature – and some don't. We're the lucky ones, you and I, aren't we?'

'Yes. We are,' said Donald, carrying the cat back to its cage. 'It's not much good my thinking of being an animal-doctor, though, sir. I think I've got to go into my father's business and be an architect. And the awful thing is, I'm no good at figures or drawing or any of the things that architects have to do. I shall be a very, very bad architect and hate every minute. And I shall keep dozens of stray animals in my backyard, just to make up for it!'

The vet laughed. 'If you want a thing badly enough, you'll get it,' he said. 'You'll be a vet one day, and be as happy as the day is long! Now to work again!'

Donald spent a very happy Sunday at the vet's. He helped him with more of the animals, he cleaned out the birds' cages, and, best of all, he took all the five dogs for a long, long walk!

The vet telephoned his parents to ask them if Donald could stay to tea with him, so he didn't need to rush home at half-past four. He went to fetch the dogs, calling 'Who's for a walk, a WALK, a WALK!' They all began to bark in delight, and the alsatian did his best to jump right over the top of his high kennel-gate!

'Take them on the hills,' said the vet. 'There will be few people there, and you can let them loose for a good run. Whistle them when you want them to come to you. *Can* you whistle, by the way?'

Donald promptly whistled so long, loudly and clearly, that the vet jumped – and all the dogs in the kennels began to bark in excitement!

'Watch out for the corgi when you're on the hills,' said the vet. 'He may not be able to keep up with the others, on his short legs. And don't lose the mongrel down a rabbit-hole – he's a terror for rabbits.'

Donald set off happily, with the five dogs gambolling round him. They might have known him for years! Once on the hills they galloped about in joy. The mongrel promptly went half-way down a rabbit-hole, and Donald had to pull him out!

A man came walking down the hill towards them. Prince, the alsatian, immediately went to

sniff at him, and the man shouted at him 'Go away!' and struck out with his stick. The big alsatian growled at once, showing all his fine white teeth.

'Call your dog off!' yelled the angry man to Donald – and the boy suddenly stopped in astonishment. Goodness – it was Mr Fairly, his schoolteacher. He whistled to the alsatian, and the dog returned to him at once – and so did the other four! They all ran to him at top speed, and milled round him in delight, whining for a pat.

Mr Fairly was astounded to see Donald – the dunce of the maths class – with five gambolling dogs! 'What in the world are you doing with this army of dogs!' he yelled. 'That alsatian's dangerous!'

'He's all right, sir!' yelled back Donald, quite pleased to have seen his fierce maths master scared of a dog. 'I'm taking them all for a walk. Heel, boys, heel!'

And, to the master's astonishment, every dog obediently rushed to Donald's heels, and walked behind as meekly as school children. Well, well – the boy might not be able to do sums – but he could manage dogs all right! What a very surprising thing! There must be more in that boy than he had ever imagined!

CHAPTER 8

Donald Gets into Trouble

In the week, Donald could only manage to go to the vet's in the evenings – and how he looked forward to the time after tea when he could slip off to the kennels and see to the dogs. They welcomed him with barks that could surely be heard half a mile away!

But poor Donald had a shock when Wednesday arrived, and the essays of the week-end came up for correction. He had handed in his smudgy, hastily written one, ashamed of it, but not having had enough time to do it again.

Mr Fairly his form master had the piles of essays in front of him, and dealt with the good ones first, awarding marks. Then he looked sternly at Donald, and waved an exercise book at him – Donald's own book!

'This essay must be written all over again!' he said. 'In fact, I'm almost inclined to say it should be written out *three* times. The spelling! The handwriting! The smudges! Donald, you should be in the lowest form, not this one! I am really ashamed to have a boy like you in my class.'

'I'm sorry, sir. I – well – I had rather a lot to do in the weekend,' said poor Donald.

'Ha yes – taking out dogs for a walk on the hills, I suppose!' said Mr Fairly. 'Well, I shall ask your parents if they will please see that your homework is done – and done well – before you go racing off with the most peculiar collection of dogs that I have ever seen!'

'Oh please, sir, don't complain to my parents!' said Donald. 'I'll rewrite the essay, sir. I'll – I'll write it out *three* times if you like!'

'Very well. Rewrite your essay three times tonight, and hand it in tomorrow,' said Mr Fairly. 'I fear, Donald, that that will mean five dogs will have to do without your company after tea!'

'The mean fellow!' thought Donald, angrily. 'He must *know* I am taking the vet's dogs walking after tea – and that's about the worst punishment he could give me – making me sit indoors, writing essays when he knows I love walking the dogs!'

But there was nothing to be done about it – Donald had to tell the vet he wouldn't be up after tea that day.

'Bad luck,' said the vet, kindly. 'The dogs will miss you. Never mind. Just come when you can. I'll manage.'

Donald sat down after tea to rewrite his essay. Blow, bother, blow! What a waste of a lovely evening! Would the dogs miss him? Would they be looking out for him? What a pity he couldn't write about *them*, instead of rewriting his stupid essay!

His mother was astonished to find him in his bedroom, writing so busily. 'I thought you would be up at the vet's,' she said. 'Are you doing extra homework, or something?'

'Well – sort of,' said Donald. His mother looked closely at what he was doing, and frowned.

'Oh Donald! You're rewriting an essay! And no wonder! *What* a mess you made of it – however could you give in work like that? I suppose you wrote it in a hurry because you give up so much time to helping the vet.'

'The weekend was so busy,' said Donald, desperately. 'I just had to hurry over my essay.'

'Well, you know what Daddy said – you can only go to help the vet if your school-work is good,' said his mother. 'I'm afraid you mustn't go any more.'

Donald stared at his mother, his heart going down into his boots. Not go any more? Not see those lovely dogs – and help with the cats and the birds? Not be with the vet again, the man he admired so much?

'I *must* go to the vet's,' he said. 'He's going to pay me for my work. I want the money for something.'

'What for?' asked his mother, astonished.

Donald looked away. How could he tell her that he had taken that little kitten to the vet's to be healed and looked after, so that he might perhaps have it for his own pet, hidden away somewhere? How could he tell her that what he earned at the vet's was to pay for the kitten's treatment? She didn't like cats. So how could she understand what he felt for the tiny kitten that had been chased and bitten by a dog?

But it was all no good. His mother told his father about his badly written essay, and he agreed that if Donald's work was poor because he hadn't enough time for it, then of course he must give up helping the vet. And what was more, he telephoned the vet himself, and told him that Donald was not coming any more.

The vet was very sorry. He liked Donald – he liked the way he did his work with the animals – he would miss him. And what about that little kitten? Well – he must find a good home for it. A pity that boy had no pets of his own – he was marvellous with animals!

Donald was very unhappy. He missed going to the vet's. He missed the companionship of all the animals, so friendly and lively. He began to sleep badly at nights.

One night he lay awake for hours, thinking of

the five dogs, the cats – and the little kitten with the half-tail. He wouldn't be able to see the kitten any more – and he somehow couldn't help feeling that it ought to belong to *him*.

He sat up in bed, and looked out towards the hill where the vet lived. 'I've a good mind to dress and go up to the kennels,' he thought. 'The dogs will know me – they won't bark. They'll be very glad to see me. *They* don't mind if I'm no good at sums or essays. I'm quite good enough for *them*. They think I'm wonderful. I'm not, of course – but it *is* so nice to be thought wonderful by *some*body!'

He dressed quickly, and slipped quietly down the stairs. He let himself out by the back door, locking it after him, and taking the key in case any burglar should try to get in.

'Now for the dogs!' he thought, feeling his heart lighter already. 'They'll be so surprised and pleased! I'll feel better after I've been with them for a little while. Oh dear – sometimes I think that dogs are nicer than people!

CHAPTER 9

In the Middle of the Night

Donald wheeled his bicycle quietly out of the shed, and was soon speeding along the dark roads, and up the hill to where the vet lived. 'I'll just have half-an-hour with the dogs,' he thought. 'I'll feel much better when I've had a word with them, and felt their tongues licking me lovingly.'

He was soon at the familiar gate, and rode in quietly. He put his bicycle into an empty shed, and went towards the kennels. Would the dogs bark, and give the alarm, telling the vet that someone was about in the night? Or would they know his footsteps, and keep quiet?

The dogs were asleep – but every one of them awoke almost as soon as Donald rode into the drive! Prince, the big alsatian, growled – and then, stopped, his ears pricked up. A familiar smell came on the wind to him – a nice, clean boy-smell – the smell of that boy who looked after him a week or so ago! The alsatian gave a little whine of joy.

The corgi was wide awake too, listening. He didn't growl. He felt sure it was the kind boy he liked so much. He tried to peer under his gate, but all he could see was the grass outside. Then he heard Donald's voice, and his tail at once began to wag.

Soon Donald was peering over the gates of the dogs' kennels. The alsatian went nearly mad with joy, but gave only a small bark of welcome, for Donald shushed him as soon as he saw him.

'Sh! Don't bark! You'll wake the vet. I'll come into each of your kennels and talk to you. I've missed you so!'

He went first into the alsatian's kennel, and the dog almost knocked him over, in his joy at seeing him. He could not help giving a few small barks of delight. He licked the boy all over, and pawed him, and rubbed his head against him. Donald stroked and patted, and even hugged him.

'It's so lovely to be with you again,' he said. 'I've missed you all so. I'm in disgrace, but *you* don't mind, do you? Now, calm down a bit – I'm going to see the other dogs. I'll come and say goodbye to you before I go!'

He left the alsatian's kennel and went to the

next one. The corgi was there, his tail wagging nineteen to the dozen, his tongue waiting to lick Donald lovingly. The boy hugged him and tickled him and rolled him over. The corgi always loved that, for he had a great sense of fun.

Then into the next kennel, where the little poodle went nearly frantic with joy. She leapt straight into his arms, and covered his face with licks. She had missed him very much. Donald sighed happily. What a lot of love dogs had to give!

Then out he went, and into the next kennel belonging to the mongrel dog. He had gone nearly mad when he had heard Donald in the other kennels, talking to the alsatian, the corgi and the poodle. He threw himself at the boy, and began to bark for joy.

'Sh!' said Donald, in alarm. 'You'll wake everybody, and I'll get into trouble. SHHH!'

The mongrel understood at once. He was a most intelligent dog, as mongrels so often are, and he certainly didn't want to get Donald into trouble. He calmed down, and contented himself with licking every single bare part of Donald he could find – knees, hands, face and neck!

'I do wish I'd thought of bringing a towel with me,' said Donald, wiping his face with his hanky. 'Now calm down – I'm going to see the labrador next door to you!'

But when he shone his torch into the next kennel, the labrador wasn't there. Another dog was there, a beautiful black, silky spaniel, the loveliest one that Donald had ever seen. He shone his torch on her, and she gave a little whine. She didn't know Donald. Who was this strange boy that all the other dogs seemed to welcome so lovingly?

'Oh – the labrador's gone back home, I suppose,' said Donald, disappointed. 'But what a lovely little thing *you* are! And oh, what have you got there – tiny puppies! Let me come in and see them. I promise not to frighten them.'

The spaniel listened to the boy's quiet voice and liked it. She gave a small whine as if to say, 'Well, come in if you like. I'm proud of my little family!'

So Donald opened the gate and went in. The spaniel was a little wary at first, but Donald knew enough of dogs to stand perfectly still for a minute while she sniffed him all over, even standing up on her hind legs to reach to his chest. Then she gave a tiny bark that meant 'Pass, friend. All's well!' and licked his right hand with her smooth tongue.

She went to her litter of tiny puppies and stood by them, looking up as if to say, 'Well? Aren't they beautiful?'

'Yes, they are. And so are you,' said Donald, stroking the smooth, silky head of the proud spaniel. 'You must be the very, very valuable spaniel that the vet told me was soon being sent to him. He said you are worth a hundred and fifty pounds, and that your puppies would be worth a lot of money, too. Oh, I wish I'd been here when you came, and could have looked after you, and cleaned your kennel and given you water.'

The spaniel curled herself round her litter of puppies, and looked up happily at Donald. He gave her one last pat. 'Goodnight. I'll leave you in peace with your little black pups.'

He went out of the kennel and saw the alsatian still standing with his paws on the top of his kennel-gate, listening for him. 'I'll just come in again and keep you company for a little while,' said the boy, and, to the dog's delight, he went into the kennel and sat down in the straw beside the big dog.

He laid his head on the dog's shoulder, and Prince sat quite still, very happy. It was warm in the kennel, and quiet. Don't go to sleep, Donald! Your eyes are shutting. Wake up, Donald, someone's coming! *Wake up!*

CHAPTER 10
A Shock for Donald!

Donald was fast asleep. He was warm and comfortable and happy. The big alsatian kept very still, glad to feel the sleeping boy so near him, his ears pricked for the slightest sound. He felt as if he were guarding Donald.

Suddenly he began to growl. It was a very soft growl at first, for he did not want to disturb the boy. But soon the growl grew louder, and awoke Donald.

'What is it? What's the matter?' he asked Prince, who was now standing up, the hackles on his neck rising as he growled even more fiercely. Then he barked, and the sudden angry noise made Donald jump.

'What's up?' he said. 'For goodness sake don't bring the vet out – he may not like my coming up here at night!'

But now the alsatian was barking without

ceasing, standing up with his feet on the gate, wishing he could jump over it. A stranger was about, and the great dog was giving warning!

'I'd better go,' thought Donald. 'If the vet comes and finds me here, he may think it was I who disturbed the dogs. Gracious, they're *all* barking now! Can there possibly be anyone about? But why? No thief could steal one of these dogs – they would fly at him at once!'

The corgi was barking his head off, and so was the mongrel dog. Even the little poodle was yapping as loudly as she could. Only the black spaniel was quiet. Perhaps she was guarding her puppies, and didn't want to frighten them?

Donald climbed over the alsatian's gate, afraid that if he opened it, the great dog would rush out, and it might be very, very difficult to get him back! He was amazed to see somebody coming out of the *spaniel's* kennel gate! There was very little moon that night, and all the boy could see was a dark figure, shutting the gate behind him.

'There's two of them!' said Donald to himself, as he saw someone else nearby. 'What are they doing? Good gracious, surely they can't be stealing the spaniel's puppies? Where's my torch? I must go to her kennel at once!'

The two dark shadows had now disappeared silently into the bushes. Donald took his torch from his pocket and switched it on. He ran to the spaniel's kennel and shone the light into it.

'The spaniel's still there,' he thought, 'Lying quite still as if she's asleep. I'd better go in and see if all her puppies are beside her.'

So in he went, and shone his torch on to the sleeping dog. Alas, alas – not one single puppy was beside her! She lay there alone, head on paws, eyes shut.

'How can she sleep with all this row going on, every single dog barking the place down!' thought Donald. 'She must be ill!'

He touched the dog – she was warm, and he felt her breath on his hands. He shook her. 'Wake up – someone has taken your puppies! Oh dear, those men must have knocked you out! They were afraid you'd bite them, I suppose! Wake up!'

But the spaniel slept on. Donald stood up and wondered what to do. The thieves had a good start now – he wouldn't be able to catch them. But wait – he knew someone who *could* trail them – someone who wouldn't stop until he had caught up with the wicked thieves!

He rushed back to the alsatian's kennel. The dog was still barking, as were all the others. 'Prince, Prince, you're to go after those men!' shouted Donald, swinging open the great gate. 'Get them, boy, get them! Run, then, RUN!'

The great alsatian shot off like an arrow from a bow, bounding along, barking fiercely. He disappeared into the darkness, the trail of the thieves fresh to his nose. Ah – wherever they had gone, wherever they hid, the alsatian would find them!

Donald suddenly found his knees shaking, and he felt astonished. 'I'm not frightened! I suppose it's all the excitement. Oh, those lovely puppies! I do hope we get them back!'

And then somebody came up at a run, and caught hold of him. 'What are you doing here? Why have you roused the dogs! You deserve to be scolded!'

It was the vet! He couldn't see that the boy he had caught was Donald. He gave him a good shaking, and Donald fell to the ground when he had finished.

'Don't, sir, don't!' he cried, struggling up. 'I'm Donald, not a thief. Sir, thieves have been here tonight and have stolen the spaniel's puppies, and . . .'

'What! Those wonderful pups!' shouted the vet, and rushed to the spaniel's kennel. He shone a powerful torch there. 'I must get the police. I heard the dogs barking, and came as soon as I could. But what on earth are *you* doing here this time of night?'

'I couldn't sleep so I just came up to be with the dogs,' said Donald. 'I know it sounds silly, but it's true. I've missed them so. And I fell asleep in the alsatian's kennel, and only woke up when the thieves came. They got away before I could do anything.'

The vet shone his torch in the direction of

Prince's kennel. 'The door's open!' he cried. 'The dog's gone!'

'Yes. I let him out, to go after the thieves,' said Donald. 'You told me once that alsatians are often used as police dogs – for tracking people – and I thought he *might* catch the thieves.'

'Donald – you're a marvel!' said the vet, and to the boy's surprise, he felt a friendly clap on his back. 'Best thing you could have done! He'll track the thieves all right – *and* bring them back here. I wouldn't be those men for anything! Now – we'll just ring up the police – and then make ourselves comfortable in Prince's kennel – and wait for him to come trotting up with those two wicked men! Ha – they're going to get a very – unpleasant – surprise!'

CHAPTER 11

GOOD OLD PRINCE!

It was very exciting, sitting in Prince's kennel in the dark, waiting for the alsatian to come back. The vet and Donald were not the only two waiting there – two burly policemen were there also!

The vet had telephoned to the police station and the sergeant and a policeman had cycled up at once, as soon as they heard what had happened. 'Good idea of that boy's, to send the dog after them,' said one man. 'Very smart. Wish *I* had a dog like that!'

The other dogs were awake and restless, especially the spaniel, who missed her puppies, and whined miserably. The men in the alsatian's kennel talked quietly, and Donald listened, half-wondering whether this could all be a dream. Then suddenly the mongrel gave a small, quiet bark.

'That's a warning bark,' said the vet, in a low tone. 'Shouldn't be surprised if Prince has found those men already, and is on his way back with them.'

Soon the other dogs barked too, and the two policemen stood up, and went silently into the dog-yard. The vet and Donald stood up too. The boy felt his knees beginning to shake with excitement again. He heard a fierce growl not far off, and a sharp bark. Yes – that was Prince all right! And what was that groaning, stumbling noise?

'That's my dog coming,' said the vet, 'and by the sound of it, he's got the men. I can hear them stumbling through the wood. I only hope they've brought back the pups.'

As the stumbling footsteps grew nearer, the police moved forward, and shone a powerful torch into the nearby bushes. The beams picked out two terrified men – and a great dog behind, his teeth bared, and a continuous growl coming from his throat – Prince, the alsatian! He had followed the trail of the men for a mile – and caught up with them! How frightened they must have been when he rounded them up!

'Stand where you are!' said the sergeant's voice, sharply. 'You're under arrest. Where are the puppies?'

'Look here – that brute of a dog has bitten

me!' said one of the men, holding out a bleeding hand. 'I want a doctor.'

'You can wait,' said the sergeant. 'A police van will be up here in a few minutes, and I'll take you down to the police station, both of you. Where are the puppies?'

'We don't know,' said the other man, sullenly. 'We dropped them when we found this dog chasing us. Goodness knows where they are!'

'That dog's a dangerous one,' said the other man, eyeing Prince carefully. 'He nipped my friend too – on the leg.'

'Serves you right,' said the vet. 'Look, sergeant, I've *got* to find those pups, or they'll all die. They need their mother. Will you see to these men, and I'll go off with Prince and see if he can find the pups for me.'

'May I come too?' asked Donald, eagerly.

'Yes. You may as well see this night's adventure to the very end!' said the vet, taking the boy's arm. 'He's done well, hasn't he, sergeant?'

'My word he has!' said the man. 'Pity he's not in the police force! Maybe you will be some day, young fellow.'

'I shan't,' said Donald. 'I'm going to be a vet. I could train police dogs for you then, if you like!'

That made everyone laugh. Then the vet gave the boy a little push. 'Come on, old son – we've got to find those puppies within an hour or so, or we may lose one or two of them – they'll be scared, and very hungry. Prince! Go find, Prince! Find my spaniel puppies.'

The black spaniel, still wide awake, was surprised at all the noise, and sad at the loss of her tiny puppies. She suddenly gave a sharp bark. 'She says she wants to come too,' said Donald.

'Right. We'll take her,' said the vet, and the

little company set off through the bushes – first Prince, the alsatian, then the vet with a basket, then Donald, then the spaniel, nosing behind.

'How will Prince know where those men threw down the puppies?' asked Donald, as they went through the woods, the vet's torch throwing a bright beam before them.

'Well, he must have passed near them, when he trailed those men,' said the vet. 'He'll remember all right. You can't beat an alsatian for tracking man or animal! Hi, Prince – don't go too fast. The spaniel can't keep up with us!'

Prince went steadily on his way, standing still at times to sniff the air. After he had gone about half a mile he stopped. The spaniel gave an excited bark and ran forward.

'Prince has smelt the pups,' said the vet. 'So has the spaniel. Don't go any further. Let her go forward to them first.'

The spaniel forced her way through the undergrowth, barking excitedly. Then she suddenly stopped and nosed something, whining in delight. The vet shone his torch on her – and there, in the grass, lay the puppies, every one of them! The mother licked them lovingly, and then looked up at the vet. She turned back and tried to pick up one of the pups in her mouth. She must carry it home!

'It's all right, old lady,' said the vet, in the

same special 'animal' voice that Donald so often used. 'It's all right. I've brought a basket, look – with a warm rug inside. You shall watch me put all the pups into it, and when I carry the basket you can walk back home with your nose touching it. They'll be safe – and you will soon be back in your kennel with them.'

And then off went a little procession through the dark woods. First, Prince, very pleased with himself. Then the vet with the basket of pups. Then the spaniel, her nose touching the basket all the time. And last of all a very happy, excited boy – Donald. *What* a night! And oh, *what* a good thing it was that he hadn't been able to sleep – and had slipped up to the kennels! Yes, Donald – that was very lucky. But you do deserve a bit of luck, you know!

CHAPTER 12
SURPRISE FOR DONALD

When the vet, Donald, and the dogs, at last arrived back at the kennels, the telephone was ringing. The vet sighed.

'I hope it's not someone to say they want me to go and look at a sick cat, or a moping monkey!' he said. 'It's still the middle of the night, and I'm tired. Aren't you, Donald?'

'I am a bit,' said Donald. 'But I don't mind. It's been – well, quite an adventurous night, hasn't it?'

The vet went to the phone. 'Hello? Yes. Who is it? Oh, Donald's father! Yes, actually, Donald *is* here. I'm sorry you were worried. Er – well, apparently he couldn't sleep, so he popped up to be with my dogs. Good thing he did, too. We've had an exciting night – been after thieves – and caught them too. Donald's been quite a hero. Well – the boy's tired out now. Shall I give him a bed for the night? Yes, yes – I'd be glad to have him. Right. Goodnight!'

'Gracious – was that Dad?' said Donald, alarmed. 'Was he very angry because I'd come up here in the middle of the night?'

'No. No, I don't think so,' said the vet. 'He seemed very relieved to know you were here, safe and sound. You get off to bed, old son. You can have the room next to mine. Don't bother about washing or anything – you're tired out. Just flop into bed.'

Donald fell asleep almost at once. He was tired out, as the vet had said, but very happy. What a good thing he had come up to the kennels – and had spotted those thieves! What a good thing that Prince had found those lovely little spaniel puppies! What a good thing that . . . but just then he fell fast asleep, and slept so very soundly that he didn't even stir until the vet came to wake him the next morning.

'Oh goodness – shall I be late for school?' said Donald, looking in alarm at his watch.

'No. Calm down. It's Saturday!' said the vet. 'Your mother's been on the phone this morning – she sounds very excited about something – I won't tell you what! She says will you please come back in time for breakfast.'

'Oh dear – I hope I'm not going to get into any more trouble!' said Donald, jumping out of bed.

'No, I don't somehow think you'll find trouble waiting for you!' said the vet. 'Buck up, though – and come back and help me today if you're allowed to.'

Donald dressed at top speed and shot home on his bicycle. Would his father be angry with him for slipping away in the middle of the night? Well – it had been worth it! It was a pity he hadn't been able to go and see if the spaniel puppies were all well and happy this morning, but maybe he could come back later on in the day.

He arrived home, put his bicycle away, and ran in through the kitchen door. Mrs Mawkins, the cook, called out to him as he came in.

'Oh there you are, Donald. Fancy you being in the papers this morning!'

Donald had no idea what she meant – but he soon knew! As soon as he went into the sitting-room, his mother ran to meet him and gave him a hug.

'Donald! Oh Donald, I didn't know I had such a brave son!'

'Well done, my boy!' said his father, and clapped him on the back. 'Fancy you being in the papers!'

Donald was astonished. He stared at his father, puzzled. 'What do you mean, Dad?'

'Well, look here!' said his father, and showed him the first page of his newspaper – and there,

right in the middle, was a paragraph all about Donald!

'Boy sends alsatian dog after thieves, in middle of night. Helps police to find priceless spaniel puppies.' And then came the story of how Donald had gone up to the kennels in the middle of the night, heard the thieves, sent the alsatian after them – and all the rest!

'I suppose the police told the paper all that last night,' said Donald, astonished. 'Mother, I couldn't sleep for thinking of those dogs, that's why I went up to them in the middle of the night. I know you and Dad said I wasn't to go and help the vet – but I did so want to see the dogs again. I just felt sort of lonely.'

'Well, all's well that ends well,' said his father, feeling really very pleased with Donald. 'Your mother and I are proud of you. We've been talking things over, and we're both agreed that you *shall* go and help the vet again . . .'

'Oh Dad! THANK you!' cried Donald, his heart jumping for joy. 'Now I'll be able to see those spaniel puppies again that the thief took. Oh, they're beautiful! Oh, I wish I was rich enough to buy one! Oh, and that little kitten too. I wish I was rich enough to pay the vet to keep it for me! I wish I could buy a . . .'

'Well now, that's enough, Donald,' said his father. 'It's no good getting big ideas, especially while your school-work is poor.'

'What about your homework for the weekend?' said his mother. 'You mustn't forget that, in all the excitement! What have you to do? Sums? An essay? Geography or history?'

'I've forgotten,' said Donald, feeling suddenly down-hearted. 'Bother it! Where did I put my exercise book? The homework I've to do for the weekend is written there. I don't feel *at all* like doing any!'

He fetched his exercise book and turned to the page where instructions for his weekend homework were written down. 'Here it is – oh blow, an *essay* again! '*Write down what you would like to be when you grow up, and give the reasons why.*' Donald stared at it in sudden delight. 'Why – I can do *that!* I want to be a vet, of course – and I know *all* the reasons why. I can put dogs and cats and horses and birds and everything into *this* essay. I'll write it at once, this *very* minute!'

CHAPTER 13

A WONDERFUL DAY

It was really very surprising to see Donald settling down so very happily to do his homework. 'We usually have such silly, dull things to write about,' he said. 'Now *this* is sensible. I've plenty to say! I only hope there are enough pages to say it in.'

It was while Donald was finishing the longest essay in his life that there came a knock at the door. It was a man from another newspaper, wanting to ask questions about Donald and his exciting night.

'I'm sorry,' said his father. 'The boy has had enough excitement. We don't want him to talk to newspaper men, and get conceited about himself.'

'Oh, I only want to ask him a few questions,' said the man. 'Such as, what does he plan to be when he's grown up? Maybe a policeman, perhaps, catching robbers and the like?'

Donald, writing his essay, heard all this. He ran to the door. 'Why – that's *exactly* what I'm writing for my weekend essay!' he said, surprised. 'I'm going to be a vet, of course. I'm putting down all my reasons. I've just finished!'

'And what are your reasons?' asked the man, smiling at Donald.

'Now listen,' said Donald's father, pushing the boy away. 'We've told you that we don't want our son to think himself too clever for words, and to get conceited! The most we'll let you do is to read what he has written.'

'Let me just have a look at it, then,' said the man. Donald handed the exercise book to him and the man glanced quickly down the essay.

'Good, good, GOOD!' he said. 'Best essay I've read for ages – straight from the heart – you mean every word of it, don't you, youngster? Do you get top marks every week for your essays? You ought to.'

'No. I'm pretty well always bottom,' said Donald. 'But this is different. It's something I *like* writing about, something I *want* to write about. I know all about a vet's work, you see. It's *grand*.'

'Go away now, Donald,' said his father, anxious not to let the boy talk too much. 'Leave your essay with me.'

Donald went off, and his father turned to the

waiting newspaper man. 'You can have this essay of his, instead of talking to him, if you like. But I think you should pay the lad for it, you know, if you want to print it. I'll put the money into the bank for him.'

'Right. Here's five pounds,' said the man, much

to the astonishment of Donald's father. 'And if that form master of his marks him bottom for *this* essay, well, all I can say is, the man doesn't know his job! I'll take it with me, have it copied, and send back the essay in time for him to take it to school next week. Thank you, sir. Good-day!'

And away went the man, looking very pleased with himself. 'Ha!' he thought, 'fancy that kid writing such an interesting piece about a vet's work, and all his animals – most remarkable! Good boy that. Deserves to have animals of his own. Funny there wasn't even a dog about the place – or a cat! Well, maybe the five pounds would help him to buy a pet for himself!'

Donald's mother and father were very proud and pleased to have been given five pounds for his essay. They went to tell Donald.

'Good *gracious*! Five pounds for a school essay!' said the boy, astounded. 'I wish I'd written it better. It isn't worth ten pence, really. And I bet I'll be bottom in class as usual! But I *say* – *five pounds*! Now – what shall I spend it on?'

'Well – I shall put it in the bank for you, of course!' said his father. The boy stared at him in dismay.

'Oh *no* Dad! I want to *spend* it – spend it on something I badly want! It's *my* money. Mother, please ask Daddy to let me have it.'

'Yes. Yes, I think you *should* have it, dear,' said

his mother, very proud of all that Donald had done the night before. 'Give it to him, Dad – we'll let him spend it on whatever he likes. He shall choose!'

'Whatever I like, Mother – do you *really* mean that?' cried Donald. 'You won't say no to *any*thing?'

'Well – you've been such a brave lad, quite a hero – and I think for once you should do as you please,' said his mother.

'Mother – if I buy a puppy with it, will you say no?' asked Donald.

'I'll say *yes*, you deserve one,' said his mother, and his father nodded his head too.

'And – suppose I asked you if I could have a little hurt kitten that the vet's keeping for me – would you mind?' asked the boy. 'It has only half a tail, because a dog bit it, so it's not beautiful – but I do love the little thing. That's really why I went to work for the vet – because he took the kitten and tended it, and kept it – and when he said he would send the bill to Dad, I said no, I'd work for him, and he could keep my earnings to pay for the kitten.'

His mother suddenly put her arms round him and gave him a warm hug.

'You can have a dog, a cat, a kitten, a monkey, anything you like! We didn't know quite what a clever son we had, nor how brave he is. We know better now. We're very very proud of you, Donald.'

'Oh *Mother*! A dog of my own – a kitten! Oh, and I might get a donkey, if I save up enough. He could live in the vet's field. And I'll buy a cage and keep budgies – blue ones and green ones. Oh, I can't believe it!'

'And if Mr Fairly, that form master of yours, gives you low marks for that fine essay, I'll have something to say to him!' said Donald's father. 'Well, well – I suppose we must now give up the idea of your being an architect when you grow up, Donald. It will be fun to have a vet in the family, for a change! I'm proud of you, son – I really am!'

CHAPTER 14

DONALD – AND HIS DOG!

Donald's father kept his word. He didn't put the five pounds into the bank – he gave it to Donald. 'Gracious – how rich I am!' said the boy, delighted. 'Mother, do you mind if I go up to see the vet – and tell him about the money?'

'Off you go!' said his mother. 'But please come back for dinner – I'm going to arrange a very special one for you!'

Donald shot off to the vet's on his bicycle. He whistled as he went, because he felt so happy. To think that last night he was so unhappy that he couldn't even go to sleep – and today he was too happy for words! All because he rushed off to see the dogs in the middle of the night!

The vet was delighted to see him again so soon – and whistled in surprise when he saw the five pound notes that the boy showed him.

'Well, well – writing must be a paying job, if you can earn five pounds for an essay!' he said. 'It takes me quite a time to earn *that* amount!'

'Sir, would you please sell me one of those beautiful spaniel puppies?' said Donald, earnestly. 'I want one more than anything in the world. A dog of my own – just imagine! Someone who'll understand my every word, who'll always know what I'm feeling and will never let me down, because he will be my very faithful friend.'

'Well, if ever a boy deserved a dog, it's you, Donald,' said the vet. 'But I'm not going to let you buy one of those pups, I'll *give* you one. I meant to, anyway, for what you did last night, and for all the help you've given me. You shall choose your own pup. Come along – let's see which one you want, before anyone else has their pick.'

Donald was speechless. His face went bright red, and the vet laughed. 'Can't you say a single word? And there's another thing – that little kitten is well enough to go now – I know you want her. You can have her too. Let her and the pup grow up together.'

'Thank you, THANK YOU!' said Donald, finding his tongue. 'But please, I've plenty of money now! I can pay for them both.'

'I know. But if you really *are* going in for animals, you'll want kennels and cages and things,' said the vet. 'I'll show you how to *make* them – much cheaper than buying them – all you'll have to do is to buy the wood and the nails. You're good with your hands – you'll enjoy making things.'

'It all seems rather like a dream,' said Donald, as they went to look at the puppies. 'I was so miserable yesterday – and today I feel on top of the world! Oh I say, aren't the puppies *lovely?* They seem to have grown since last night. That little fellow is trying to crawl!'

The spaniel's mother looked up at them out of beautiful brown eyes. With her nose she gently pushed one of the puppies towards Donald. 'That's the one she wants you to have!' said the vet. 'It's the best of the lot.'

And that is the one Donald chose. He left it with the mother till it was old enough to be his – and now he is making a fine kennel for it! 'It will be yours when you are old enough,' he tells the puppy. 'I expect the kitten will sometimes sleep in your kennel with you, so I'll bring her along soon so that you can make friends.'

He went to tell his Granny about the dog he had chosen. She listened, very pleased. 'Well, well – I meant to give you a puppy myself, for your birthday, if your mother said yes – and now you have won one for yourself, by working for the vet. You deserve a dog, Donald, and I know you'll train him well. I can't give you a dog, now you have one – so I think I'll buy you a really good dog basket, so that you can have him in your room at night, to guard you when you're asleep!'

'That puppy is going to be very lucky!' said Donald. 'I'm making him a *lovely* kennel – the vet's helping me. We went and bought the wood together, out of the money I won for that essay. I've a kitten too – the one whose tail was half-bitten off by a dog. And I *think* I'm going to breed budgerigars, Granny. I've still enough money out of my five pounds to buy a breeding-cage. I'm going to give *you* my first baby budgie. Would you like a green or a blue one?'

'Oh – a green one, I think,' said Granny. 'It will match my curtains! Bless you, Donald – you do deserve your good luck. You earned it yourself – and that's the best good luck there is!'

Donald still goes up to help the vet, of course, and you should have seen him one week when the vet was ill! He looked after all the dogs, the cats, the birds – and a little sick monkey! How happy and proud he was! How good it felt to go round and see every animal, big or small, look up in delight when he came . . . Yes, Donald – you'll be a fine animal-doctor, when the time comes!

Prince, the alsatian, has gone back to his own

home now, of course – but Donald often sees him when he goes out. Prince always sees him first, though! Donald suddenly hears a soft galloping noise behind him – and then he almost falls over as the big alsatian flings himself on the boy, whining and licking, pawing him lovingly.

'Do you still remember that exciting night in the dark woods?' says Donald, ruffling the thick fur round the dog's neck. 'Remember those little spaniel puppies? Do you see this beautiful black spaniel at my heels – he was one of the pups we rescued that night, you and I! I chose him for myself. *Dear* old Prince. I'll never forget you!'

One day you may meet a boy walking over the grassy hills somewhere – a boy with five or six dogs round him, dogs that come at his slightest whistle. It will be Donald, taking out the kennel-dogs for the vet, letting them race and leap and play to their hearts' content. Call out to him – 'DONALD! Which is *your* dog?'

But you'll know which it is without his telling you – that silky black spaniel beside him. What's its name? Well, call 'Bonny, Bonny, Bonny' and it will come rushing over to you at once!

Goodbye, Donald. Goodbye, Bonny. Good luck to you both. You deserve it!

Enid Blyton titles available at Bloomsbury Children's Books

Adventure!

Mischief at St Rollo's
The Children of Kidillin
The Secret of Cliff Castle
Smuggler Ben
The Adventure of the Secret Necklace

Happy Days!

The Adventures of Mr Pink-Whistle
Run-About's Holiday
Bimbo and Topsy
Hello Mr Twiddle
Shuffle the Shoemaker
Mr Meddle's Mischief
Snowball the Pony
The Adventures of Binkle and Flip

Enid Blyton Age-Ranged Story Collections

Best Stories for Five-Year-Olds
Best Stories for Six-Year-Olds
Best Stories for Seven-Year-Olds
Best Stories for Eight-Year-Olds

WIN A WEEKEND BREAK FOR YOUR FAMILY AT CENTER PARCS

THE COMPETITION WILL BE JUDGED BY ENID BLYTON'S DAUGHTER, GILLIAN BAVERSTOCK, AND THE FIVE LUCKY WINNERS WILL BE ANNOUNCED ON THE 19TH AUGUST 1997.

HOW TO ENTER

1. Solve the riddle:

   My first is in apple and also in pear
   My second's in rabbit but never in hare
   My third is in lucky but not in thirteen
   My fourth is in runner and also in bean ____________
   My fifth is in tortoise and also in snail
   My last is in bucket but never in pail
   My whole is a pleasure to go on together
   But better watch out for the wasps and the weather!

2. Now describe the most amazing adventure you've ever had (using no more than 30 words):

____

____

____

____

____

____

Please send your entries on this form to the following address:
Blyton/Center Parcs Competition
Bloomsbury Publishing Plc, 38 Soho Square, London W1V 5DF.

Name: ______________________________ Age: __________

Address: ______________________________________

____

Telephone Number: ______________________________

Signature of a parent/responsible adult: ______________________

The competition is open to any child of twelve years and under and resident in the U.K.
All entries must be signed by a parent or guardian.
See overleaf for Terms and Conditions.

CLOSING DATE FOR ENTRIES: 31ST JULY 1997.

Terms and Conditions

1. Bloomsbury Publishing Plc cannot take any responsibility for the return of any entries to the competition.

2. The competition is open to any child of twelve years and under and resident in the U.K, subject to signature of parent or guardian. No employees of Bloomsbury Publishing Plc, Center Parcs or their agents are eligible to enter the competition.

3. The prizes for winning entries will be the ones specified only. They may not be changed and are non-transferable. No substitute prizes or cash alternatives are available. The prizes consist of the use of a 3-bedroom villa for a family of up to 6 at a UK Center Parcs Village, plus £150 worth of Center Parcs' vouchers which can be spent in the Village. It does not include any additional charges such as meals, insurance, sports & leisure activities or other personal expenses. Travel expenses are covered up to the value of £50 per prize. Bookings are subject to availability and to the terms and conditions published in Center Parcs' brochure.
   The prizes should be taken by Spring 1998.

4. All entries must be received by 31st July1997. All entries must be submitted using this competition page, photocopies will not be accepted. Incomplete, illegible, spoilt or late entries will not be considered.

5. The prizes will be awarded to the entrants who have correctly solved the riddle and, in the judge's opinion, have submitted the most apt, original and amazing adventure. All entries will be judged by Gillian Baverstock. Her decision is final and no correspondence will be entered into.

6. Winners will be notified by post or telephone, no later than Monday 11th August. The winners will be required to attend a party on 19th August 1997 to announce the prizes to the press, they may also be required to attend picture-taking for publicity purposes without compensation, other than reasonable out of pocket expenses.

7. Details of winners and results will be available by post after 11th August. If required please send a stamped, self-addressed envelope to Blyton/Center Parcs Competition, Bloomsbury Publishing Plc, 38 Soho Square, London, W1V 5DF.

8. All entry instructions form part of the rules and the submission of an entry will be deemed to signify acceptance of these rules by the entrant. Closing date for entries 31st July 1997.

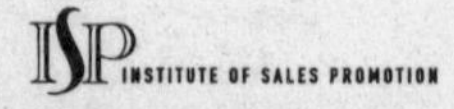

ISP Registration Number: 658
Rules conform to the Institute of Sales Promotion recommended practice.